How Tables Came To Umu Madu

The Fabulous History of an Unknown Continent

by
Chief-Dr.-Gen.-Prof. Efanim Ekeh
(Inyanga the First of Uwa Dum)

Africa World Press, Inc.
P.O. Box 1892
Trenton, New Jersey 08607

AFRICA WORLD PRESS, INC.
P. O. BOX 1892
TRENTON, NJ 08607

FIRST PRINTING 1989

Copyright © Africa World Press, Inc.

All rights reserved. No part of this publication may be reproduced, stored in a retrieval system or transmitted in any form or by any means electronic, mechanical, photocopying, recording or otherwise without the prior written permission of the publisher.

Illustrated by Thomas Hamilton

Cover Design and typesetting by
Deanne Bauer of
Apostrophes Bookshop, New York

Library of Congress Catalog Card Number: 88-83368

ISBN: 0-86543-127-2 Cloth
        0-86543-128-0 Paper

Disclaimer

All the characters and locations in this book are real. Resemblances to actual persons and places are fully intended. However, a few names have been changed to protect the guilty.

Chapter One

Umu Madu in The Good Old Days

There was once a village called Umu Madu, where the people loved to have feasts. Every chance the villagers had, they called a feast to celebrate one thing or another.

"There is a new moon in the sky," the people of Umu Madu would say sometimes. "Let us have a feast to celebrate it."

"The moon is now full," the villagers might say a few weeks later. "Let us have a feast to celebrate the full moon."

At the beginning of the farming season, after they had planted their crops, the people of Umu Madu had a feast.

In the middle of the farming season, after the rains had started and the farms were green with growing crops, the people of Umu Madu held a feast.

At the end of the farming season, after the crops had been harvested and placed in the barns, the people of Umu Madu had a feast.

Sometimes even when nothing happened, the people of Umu Madu had a feast. If anyone asked them what the feast was for, they replied: "We are having this feast because nothing has happened."

Some of the feasts were small and some were big, but always there was a feast in the village of Umu Madu, and all the feasts were long and happy.

🚶 A Feast for All 🚶

All the feasts were held under the big cottonwood tree in the middle of the market clearing at the center of the village of Umu Madu. The men killed the chickens or the goats or a cow, depending on how big the feast was. They also cut up the meat and cooked it in big iron pots, which they stirred with long sticks. The women cooked the soup and the stew as well as the rice and the fufu. Children fetched water or firewood and darted here and there on errands for the adults.

When everything was ready, the elders of Umu Madu appointed four or five young men to divide the food, so that every man, woman and child would get a share. Fufu and rice were piled high on everyone's plate. Big pieces of meat stuck out above the surface of everyone's stew and soup. However, the heart of the feast was the big lumps of meat which were spread out in long rows on banana leaves or raffia mats. From the oldest man to the youngest child, the people of Umu Madu chose their shares of meat according to their ages.

For as long as anyone could remember, the people of Umu Madu had always eaten their feasts on the ground. Some people squatted on the ground. Some people knelt on the ground. Some people sat on the ground.

No Skin Arrives—A Truly Strange Stranger

Then one day a stranger arrived in the village of Umu Madu.

This was not the first time a stranger had come to Umu Madu. However, this stranger was very strange. No one had ever seen or heard anyone like him before. The villagers nicknamed the stranger No Skin because his skin had no color. No Skin had hair which looked like corn silk and eyes which shone like glass beads. At first everyone thought he had no toes, until he took off his shoes and allowed some of the villagers to count his toes. He had ten of them.

"Urupirisi. Urupirisi. Urupirisi," No Skin said to the villagers of Umu Madu. When someone was found who could understand No Skin's language, what he was saying was: "What have we here? Why are intelligent people like you eating their feast on the ground?"

"We have always eaten our feasts on the ground," the villagers replied. "Where do you want us to eat? On the tree tops or in the sky?"

"Haven't you ever heard of tables?" No Skin asked.

"No," the villagers replied, surprised and a little ashamed. "We have never heard of tables. What are tables?"

No Skin began describing a table to the people of Umu Madu. He drew a picture of a table on the ground for them as he said: "My friends, these are modern times. If you want to be modern and up-to-date, you must stop eating on the ground and start eating on tables."

"Where can we find a table?" the villagers begged. "We do not want to be left behind by progress. We want to be modern and up-to-date."

"No problem," No Skin replied. "Send along four able-bodied men with me, and they will bring back a table to the village within a week."

Umu Madu Gets a Table

Within a week, just as No Skin had promised, there was a table in the village of Umu Madu. It was big and long and heavy, and the villagers spent many hours admiring it, walking around it, rubbing their hands on it and smiling at their reflections on its shiny top.

"This table is so good," the elders of the village said, "That we cannot wait until the next feast several weeks from now to try it. Let us have a feast at once and try the new table."

Everyone thought that was a good idea.

So a feast was called immediately. Two cows were killed. Fufu and rice were cooked in abundance. Everyone in the village came out to enjoy the big feast on the new table. No one bothered about raffia mats and banana leaves anymore.

However, as the young men who had been appointed by the elders began to divide the meat, they made a disturbing discovery. There was not enough space around the table for everyone.

"We have a problem here," one old man said. "How are we going to solve it?"

"Why don't the elders go into a conference with one another, as is our custom," someone suggested. "Let the elders tell us what to do about this problem."

"Yes, yes," everyone agreed. "Let the elders decide for us."

So the elders went into a conference. After a long time, they came back to the assembly and announced: "We cannot agree on how to satisfy everyone about the table. We cannot agree who should eat at the table and who should not. So we have decided instead to return the table to No Skin, so we can continue our unity and eat our feasts on the ground together, as we have always done. If we cannot find No Skin, we can put the table away, and he can take it back whenever he comes this way again."

"No-o-o-oh!" many members of the assembly shouted. There was a lot of murmuring and grumbling.

Then, one young man said: "We now have the table, and everyone agrees it is a good thing. Would it not be foolish to let it sit idle? Would it not be even more foolish to give it back to No Skin . . . All members of the assembly of Umu Madu who agree with me, please say Hay-ay-ay!"

"Hay-ay-ay!" everyone in the assembly seemed to shout.

The Table Creates Discontent

The elders were surprised and disappointed. Not often did the community assembly fail to heed their advice. "Alright," the elders said, "if that is the will of Umu Madu, then so be it. However, we will choose positions around the table according to age. Old people will choose first. People of Umu Madu, show that you agree with us by saying Hay-ay-ay!"

"Hay-ay-ay!" most voices shouted.

However, there were some voices which said "No!"

The Village of Umu Madu liked to do things by having everyone agree. So the elders said, "If we cannot do it by age, how then shall we do it?"

One young man raised his hand and was given permission to speak.

"The times we live in are modern times," the young man said. "Modern times and modern things like the table are for the young. So I say, the young men should eat at the table. The elders can eat on the ground. Everyone who agrees with me say "Hay-ay-ay!"

"Hay-ay-ay!" most of the young people shouted.

"No-o-oh!" most of the older people shouted.

The village of Umu Madu was faced with one of the sharpest disagreements its community assembly had ever seen. The elders looked at one another, shook their heads and scratched them. Then one elder cleared his throat and said:

"Perhaps we can do it by volunteering. Perhaps some people will volunteer to eat on the ground."

Everyone thought that was a good idea. However when the elder said, "Who will volunteer to eat on the ground?" people began to answer "Someone else."

"Who else?" the elders asked.

"Anyone else but me," everyone said.

At this point, the elders decided to go into another conference. For a long time and after many debates they still could not agree on what to do. In the end, they decided to settle the matter by drawing sticks. Anyone who drew a short stick would eat on the ground. Anyone who drew a long stick would eat at the table.

Feasts Turn to Fights

However, by the time the elders returned from their conference to announce their decision the people were pushing, shoving and fighting for places around the table.

"Shame!" the elders cried in dismay. "Shame, Umu

Madu, shame!"

When the fighting stopped, the elders said, "Alright, alright, if this is what we have been driven to, then let everyone keep the place he now has. Those of you who have occupied places around the table, keep your places. Those of you who are on the ground, stay on the ground. But please stop fighting like hyenas. We came here to feast not to fight."

That was how the matter was settled for that day. However it did not end there. Disunity had come to the feasts of Umu Madu, because when there was a feast some people ate at the table and some people on the ground. Envy had come to the feasts of Umu Madu. Those who ate on the ground looked enviously or rolled their eyes at those who ate at the table. Pride had come to the feasts of Umu Madu. Those who ate at the table stuck up their noses in the air and looked down on those who ate on the ground. Unhappiness had come to the feasts of Umu Madu. For the first time ever, everyone was not happy at the feasts.

Every feast that the people of Umu Madu held now ended in a fight. People came to the feasts not just to enjoy themselves but to fight for places around the table. Those who had eaten on the ground during the last feast thought it was their turn to eat at the table this time.

Feasts turn to fights

However, those who had eaten at the table the last time thought they should do so again.

"Once a person has fought to get a place by the table," some of the villagers said, "he should keep it permanently."

Some villagers even felt that once a person had begun to eat at the table, his wives and children should also eat at the table, and even his children and his children's children, whenever they were born, should have the future right to eat at the table.

Some villagers became so angry at what was going on that they refused to attend any more feasts.

Then one day just before a very big feast, someone secretly sawed more than halfway through one of the table's legs. In the middle of the feast, when the meat and all other goodies had been heaped on the table, the leg broke, the table tipped over, and all the meat fell to the ground.

Various people accused one another of the trick. A big free-for-all fight broke out. Pots were broken. Basins of rice were kicked over. The meat was trampled underfoot.

Tables Are Abolished

The day after the big fight, the elders called everyone together in the market clearing. "Umu Madu," the elders said, "the table which No Skin gave us has been nothing but trouble. There is only one way to solve our problem—destroy the table before it destroys us."

"Hay-ay-ay!" the whole assembly responded in unison. "Let us destroy the table before it destroys us!"

The men, women and children of Umu Madu went home and got their axes, machetes, clubs and pestles and set upon the table and smashed it to pieces.

"Now we can be one again," one elder said, after the task was done.

"Yes," another elder replied. "We can eat our feasts in unity and harmony once again."

"Yes," someone else in the assembly said. "Let us call a feast immediately to celebrate our freedom from the table."

"Yes, yes," everyone agreed.

A date was set for the special feast. Three cows were killed. Banana leaves and clean raffia mats were laid out on the swept ground, as in the old days. This was going to be the biggest and happiest feast Umu Madu had ever had.

Individual Table Owners Assert Their Rights

However, just as the feast was about to start, someone pointed out that a few villagers had brought their own little, private tables to the feast.

"Why?" the elders asked. "Did we not agree to eat

together on the ground as we used to do before No Skin brought the table?"

"We agreed! Yes, we agreed!" a majority of the assembly replied.

"Why then have some people brought tables?" the elders asked.

"I now like tables," one table owner said. "I found No Skin, and he said I can have my own table if I wish. So, since I enjoy eating at a table, why shouldn't I be able to do so?"

"Me too," another table owner said. "I not only like tables, but I have become so used to them that I can no longer bear to eat my meals on the ground."

Other table owners gave similar answers.

"You must destroy the tables," the elders commanded, "so that we can have harmony and unity as of old."

"My table is mine to do with as I please," one table owner said in an insulting voice. "It cost me plenty of money. No one can destroy it."

Another table owner agreed with the first one. He said, "If I cannot eat my part of the feast on my table, then I will not share in the feast at all!"

So, the big feast which was supposed to bring back peace and harmony to Umu Madu instead brought disharmony and discord. There was first a long argument and then a big fight, during which many bones were broken. Since that day harmony and unity left the village and have not returned.

Chapter Two

 The Table Wars

Tables. Tables. Tables. Tables. Tables. The people of Umu Madu appeared to have gone crazy about tables. They talked about tables, dreamed about tables, and beat their wives about tables. They quarrelled about tables, fought about tables, and fomented witchcraft against their neighbors about tables. It seemed that tables were all they lived for—high tables, low tables, square tables, round tables, tables with three legs, tables with four legs, tables that were shaky and tables that were sturdy. When villagers met on the roads, instead of asking each other: "How are your wives and children?" they asked instead: "How are your tables?" When babies first learned to talk, the first word they said no longer was "Daa" or "Dede," but "Babel."

When things were truly out of hand, the Council of Elders met secretly and decided to do something drastic to solve the problem. They planned to call a big feast and invite all the people to bring all their tables. In the middle of the feast, the elders would smash every single table that was brought to the market clearing that day.

However, even though the elders had sworn themselves to the strictest secrecy, word of their plan leaked out. A group of hot-headed young men who loved tables met and decided to summon a general meeting of the village. No one had ever before heard of youth calling an assembly of the village, but there were many things going on now that no one had ever heard of before.

How Everyone Became Abolished

At the meeting the young men accused the elders of "wanton duplicity" and "nefarious conspiracy." Someone made a motion to abolish the Council of Elders. Eyebrows were raised. Abolish the Council of Elders, which had always ruled the village for as far back as anyone could remember? Even though many people were chagrined by the idea, the motion nevertheless carried on a narrow vote. The Council of Elders was abolished and would henceforth be replaced by a Youth Council. There were loud cheers.

But how would the members of the Youth Council be selected? There was never a problem selecting members of the Council of Elders. The oldest men in the village became its members automatically. If the same principle were followed, then babies, being the youngest, should be members of the Youth Council. This, of course, was unacceptable. Also, what would happen in the future as members of the Youth Council got older and began to grow grey hair? Would they be expelled?

These and many other questions which arose were not answered. Nevertheless, the loudest and strongest-eyed young men managed to get themselves elected members of a Special Committee of the Youth Council. From that day onwards, the Special Committee would have the last say in all village affairs.

The following day, the Council of Elders met and abolished the Youth Council and declared that henceforth all members of the Special Committee were ostracized.

The Special Committee then met and abolished the Council of Elders for the second time and declared all its members ostracized.

The village was thrown into confusion. Angry words and abuses and insults were thrown wildly about. Because an elder was most likely someone's grandfather or father or uncle or older brother, and because a youth was most likely someone's younger brother or son or grandson or nephew, the problem grew into a big ball of sticky wax. From being an issue between the young and the old, it soon became a problem between everyone and everyone else. Alliances were formed, re-aligned, broken and reformed. Fights broke out, then battles, then full-scale wars.

After The Table Wars

These were the wars which became known in history as the Table Wars. They lasted many years, and while they were in progress, the people of Umu Madu had no time to plant their crops or stake their yams or weed their cassava plots. The little they planted rotted in the ground because they had no time to harvest it. What did not rot was consumed by termites.

Nearly half of the people of Umu Madu were killed during the Table Wars. Half of the half that did not die by the machete or spear or arrow starved to death. The remainder were so emaciated and weak that they could hardly stand up, let alone throw a spear or pull a bowstring. For a very long time, hardly a sound came out of the village of Umu Madu.

However, after sometime—a very long time—a semblance of life returned to the village. The farms became green again with crops. During the day the work songs of men and women filled the air again. In the evenings,

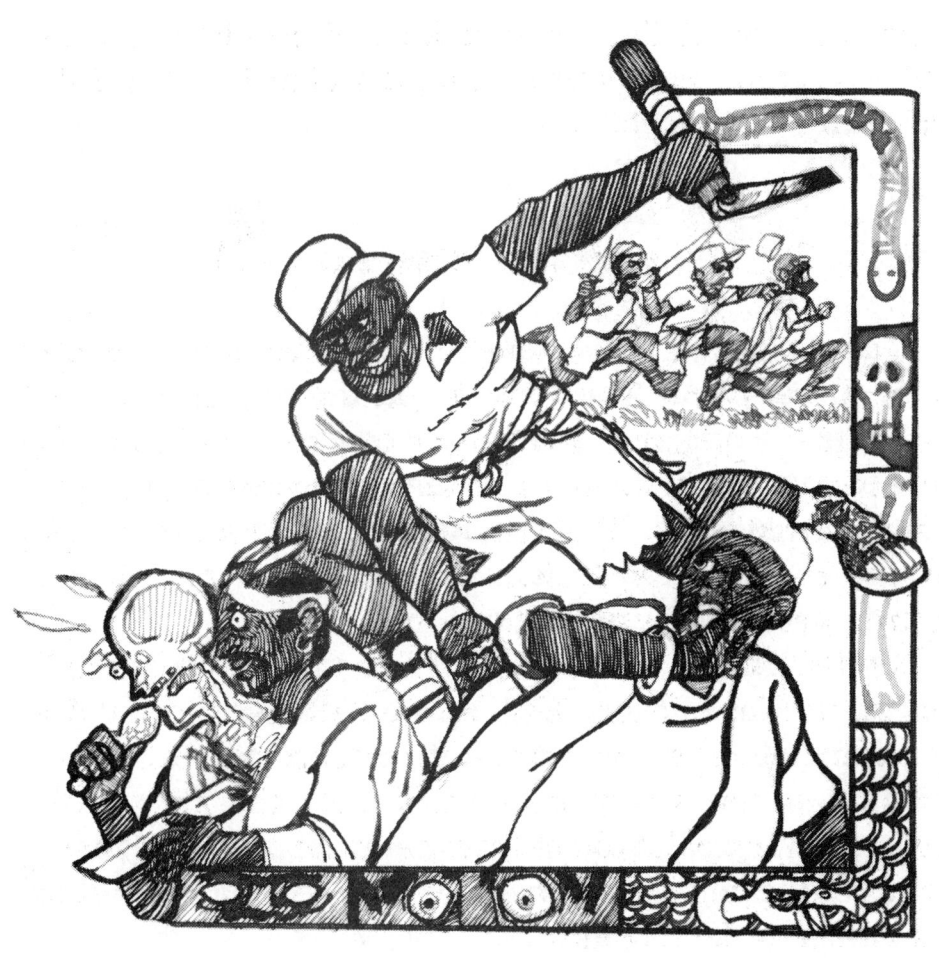

Table wars

one again could see blue supper smoke curling into the sky from the kitchens and hear the sounds of pestles pounding into mortars. Oily lips and fingers returned to the men. Round bellies came back to the children. Even the dogs were fed and stopped chasing other people's chickens.

Then tables came back—again! Actually tables had never entirely left the village. During the Table Wars, most of them had been broken and their legs used to smash the heads of opponents. However, a common practice had been to consider tables as war trophies. When you killed a man, you took his wives and tables as booty. As a result, men who survived the war acquired many wives and many tables.

As the village of Umu Madu returned to prosperity and memories of the wars began to fade, some people began to suggest that it might be a good idea to have common feasts again.

"Never again!" most people shouted at first. However, people began to remember how the feasts used to be in the old days before the Table Wars. As the farming season began and there was no feast, and the farming season ended and there was no feast, and the bright slice of new moon rose in the sky and there was no feast and the round full moon lavished its light on the village and still there was no feast, people began to say cautiously: "We could perhaps try having feasts again. Perhaps."

"But the feast must be on the ground," some of the villagers suggested, "so that we don't again have the problems that tables used to bring."

"No way," another group of villagers insisted. "The era B.T. (Before Tables) was the era of darkness and primitivity. We have passed that era now and cannot go back to it. Tables are here to stay."

The latter group prevailed. The next question was about the shape and size of the table. It was agreed that there should just be one table big enough to accommodate every man, woman and child in the village. Since no one knew how to build such a table, the villagers of Umu Madu decided to find No Skin and seek his advice.

The Man Called Trader-and-Traveler

At this time in the village, there was a man known as T-and-T (for Trader-and-Traveler), although many preferred to call him by his other nickname, which was Ogasi-Ahugh-Ahu-Ekwu. T-and-T had a reputation of having traveled everywhere. He claimed to know where No Skin lived, high on a hill, and across a big lake with

The man called Trader-and-Traveler

no shores. T-and-T said that for a fee he would take a delegation of villagers to see No Skin about the table.

As soon as the plan was agreed upon, everyone wanted to be part of the delegation. The first delegation went. Then the second delegation went. Then the third and fourth and fifth and sixth. Then the twentieth. The same curious thing happened again and again. Delegations always went but never returned, except for T-and-T, who always told the same story. "On the way back," he always said, "the others took a different route and I took a different route. They must have become lost."

"How could so many sensible men keep getting lost?" many villagers wondered. "And how come T-and-T always parted company with them and never got lost himself?"

Rumors began to circulate that T-and-T and some other traders had a conspiracy to tie up the people who went with him on delegations and put them on big canoes which took them across the big lake to where No Skin lived. There, according to these rumors, they became No Skin's laborers and servants and worked on his large farms. However, these were just rumors.

The grumbling in the village became quite loud after some time. A decision was made to summon T-and-T and demand an accounting for all the delegations that had left with him but had never returned. If necessary, the village was going to squeeze T-and-T's throat until the truth came out of him. However, on the appointed day T-and-T disappeared.

A Table-Times-Seven Comes to Umu Madu

Chapter Three

 The Mirror Of Truth

No Skin Returns

Then one day No Skin suddenly appeared in the market clearing at the center of the village. Beside him, smiling coyly, was T-and-T, who had learned No Skin's language and therefore became his interpreter. The whole village of Umu Madu assembled, including the women and children.

No Skin sat on a high chair between two tarpaulin tents which he had erected with T-and-T's help.

"You have problems," No Skin said through his interpreter.

"Yes," the villagers replied. "We have problems."

"I can see you are sad and unhappy," No Skin said.

"Yes, we are sad and unhappy," the villagers agreed.

"You are confused and mystified," No Skin said.

"Yes," the villagers said in reply. "We are confused and mystified."

"And you want a big table for your community feasts," No Skin incanted.

"Yes, we want a table for our feasts," the villagers chorused.

"Alright," No Skin said.

"Alright," the villagers repeated, but then No Skin told them that it was not necessary to echo everything he said.

"In due time, you will get your table," No Skin said.

The villagers began clapping and cheering.

 ## The Mirror Of Truth

"However," No Skin said, waving his hands wildly in the air to interrupt them. "However, the table is only a symptom and not the cause of your problems. In order to show you the real cause of your problems, I have arranged a small demonstration. Over here to my left is a tent, as you can see. Inside it is something called THE MIRROR OF TRUTH. I want each of you to go into that tent, look in the mirror and then come out and tell the rest of the assembly what you saw. Now, who would like to be the first to go in?"

There was a rush. People were knocked down and shoved aside and a few children were nearly trampled.

"It doesn't matter. It doesn't matter," No Skin said.

"Everyone will get a chance to peer into THE MIRROR OF TRUTH."

The first man to go into the tent shrieked in terror and dashed out again. "No! No! No!" he gasped breathlessly. "You should see it. No, you don't want to see it! It is fearsome. It is ugly! A big gorilla, dark as midnight. No, it is like ten gorillas rolled into one. Its teeth are longer than my fingers."

"You looked in the mirror and what you saw was a giant ape?" No Skin asked.

"Yes, yes!" the man replied, holding his hand to his wildly thumping heart. "A big, black ape!"

"The rest of you may now take your turns," No Skin said.

One by one the people of Umu Madu filed into the tent. Each person came out terrified speechless about the giant ape in the trick mirror. There were some who did not want to go in after they heard the terrified shrieks of the others, but No Skin kept telling them, "Come on. Come on. Move it along." In the end, after the last child had taken his turn, No Skin addressed the assembly:

"You should all know by now why you are sad and confused," he said. "The reason is simple. You are all apes, trying to be like people!"

"What!!!???" the assembly cried out in unison.

"Whom are you abusing? Whom are you calling apes?" Several men leaped to their feet and grabbed their machetes. One man threw a spear, but No Skin dodged. One man smashed a nearby table against the ground and grabbed one of its legs as a weapon.

"You see? You see?" No Skin said undaunted. "Your very behavior right now proves my point. THE MIRROR OF TRUTH does not lie . . . " He was still in the middle of a sentence when several men rushed at him.

 The Deadly Iron Stick

What happened in the next few moments was magic to the eyes. No Skin pulled a short iron object out of his pocket and pointed it at the man who had come nearest to him. The iron spat fire, and the man fell dead to the ground. Five more times the iron object spat fire, and five more men were on the ground dead or dying.

Horror took over the assembly. Eyes were wide with wonder and fear.

"Now," No Skin said, "Do you see how convincing truth can be?" He placed the smoking convincer carefully across his knees as he talked, and every time it seemed someone did not believe him, he fingered it just a little bit and immediately the person believed him completely.

"THE MIRROR OF TRUTH does not lie," No Skin said once again. "You are what each of you saw in the mirror." He paused to ask: "Are there any questions?" A few daring souls cleared their throats, but no one asked any questions. "Well then," No Skin continued. "Luckily for you what you are you do not have to be forever. But there are some things you must do first."

No Skin and His Deadly Iron Stick

"What must we do?" the villagers asked eagerly.

"You believe me then?" No Skin asked.

"Yes, yes, we believe you," the villagers replied.

"In that case," No Skin said, "you already have the first thing you must have—Faith. Do you know what Faith is?"

"No," the villagers of Umu Madu said. "We do not know what Faith is."

"Faith," No Skin said, "is believing what you are told no matter what. It is believing without seeing. It is the evidence of things which appear not. Do you understand all that?"

"Yes, yes," the villagers of Umu Madu agreed, mystified but not daring to admit it.

The Mirror Of Faith

"Alright," No Skin said, agreeing with himself. "Over here to my right is another tent with a mirror in it. I want you to queue up and take turns looking at yourselves in this mirror."

The people gasped and shook their heads as they shrank away. No one was eager to look at another mirror.

"Come on, come on," No Skin urged them. "You there with the big nose and thick lips," he said, pointing at one man. "Why don't you be the first." The man in question tried to avoid No Skin's eyes and to back away into the crowd. No Skin stared sternly at him and fingered the iron object on his knee, and the man stumbled forward, holding one hand over his face and peering between his fingers.

Once inside the tent the man began to shout for joy. "Wow! Whee! Yay-yay! Ha-a-a-ah!" His uncontrolled dancing nearly knocked down the tent. The crowd outside became puzzled and curious.

"Enough time taken, " No Skin said to the man in the tent. "Come out right now!"

The man did not come out but continued to chant with joy inside the tent.

"Pull him out," No Skin said to T-and-T, who reached into the tent and dragged the man out.

The man would not stop dancing and shouting for joy. It took several minutes before he could be made to speak coherently. The first thing he said was "I am going to be a chief! I will be rich and have a big house and fine clothes. I looked so beautiful that I did not recognize myself in that mirror. Such rich clothes. Ornaments of gold and silver. Wives without number. I saw it all in the mirror . . ."

"Alright," No Skin said. "That is what Faith does for you. It transforms you into something beautiful, no matter your previous condition."

By now the rest of the villagers were rushing to get into the tent, and were restrained only when No Skin picked up his iron stick. The stick spat fire one more time, and the man who had just come out of the tent fell dead to the ground.

 ## Umu Madu Learns To Obey

"Now," No Skin said. "That is Lesson Number Two. Obedience. I told that man to come out of the tent and he did not obey me instantly: If you want to be rescued from your backward nature, first you must have Faith. Secondly you must obey, do what you are told as soon as you are told. Obedience was the first law in heaven."

A chill fell on the assembly as the people watched the seventh man die that day before their eyes. No one was now eager to go into the tent. However, when No Skin shouted "Next!" they all remembered the recent lesson about Obedience. So one by one they filed into the tent, and each person came out smiling and laughing and clapping his hands and making other signs of joy. Each of them saw himself or herself in the mirror as a chief or a chief's wife or a prince or a princess.

After the last child had gazed in THE MIRROR OF FAITH, No Skin descended from his high chair, and wiping the sweat off his face, said askance: "This country of yours is too blasted hot! Enough business for one day. We still have not solved your problem with the Community Table, but that must wait till another day. By the way, how many lessons did you learn today?"

"Two," one forward boy of about fourteen shouted eagerly. "Faith and Obedience."

No Skin's iron stick spat fire, and the boy fell dead. "There were three lessons," No Skin said.

"Yes, yes, we learned three lessons," the villagers echoed, even though they could remember only two.

"First lesson you learned is that your problems are caused by your trying to rise above your basic nature. Second lesson is Faith. Third lesson is Obedience."

In the meantime one man, who was trying to get ahead in life by ingratiating himself with No Skin, had climbed a coconut tree. Now, he cut open one coconut, and grinning fawnishly offered a cold drink to No Skin. No Skin drank down the juice eagerly. Then he shot the man for seeking attention.

The villagers were equally horrified and mystified. "Wow! Chai God! Odi egwu!" they muttered as they trudged home. They had never seen anything like this before. Perhaps No Skin was a god. He was powerful and unpredictable and arbitrary, just like gods. Only he knew the answers to his own questions.

Chapter Four

 Umu Madu Goes To School

Will No Skin Come Again?

For years no one heard from No Skin again. Rumors came and went about if and when he was coming back. Various would-be prophets said he was coming back next year, next month or next week. Some said he would return by land, by sea or by air. Quite simply, No Skin did not return any time or in any medium.

T-and-T, who knew more about No Skin than anyone else in the village, became very important and rich as people came to his house daily to seek his opinion about No Skin's return. T-and-T charged one manila and a cock to render an opinion. Smiling cagily, as if he knew more than he was revealing, T-and-T told everyone the same thing, after beating about ten bushes, namely, "A wise and prudent man is always prepared. No Skin will return one day soon."

Everyone heeded T-and-T's advice by reciting the lessons all of them had learned during his last visit. "We are sad and unhappy," they recited. "We are confused and mystified. We want a big table for our community feasts. The table, however, is only a symptom and not the cause of our problem. The real cause of our problem was revealed to us by THE MIRROR OF TRUTH. We are apes trying to be like people. THE MIRROR OF TRUTH does not lie. Only faith will save us from our bestial fate. Faith will transform us all into chiefs, princes and princesses and make all of us rich. We must always do what we are told, because obedience was the first law in heaven."

Umu Madu were like people hypnotized. At the farm and on their way to the river the people recited the lessons. They became work songs for men and festival songs for the women and moonlight *oro* songs for the children.

No Skin Returns

Then one morning No Skin appeared unannounced in the market clearing. The tom-tom sounded an emergency call and all the villagers left whatever they were doing and rushed to the market clearing. The Council of Elders gave No Skin a big ram and a he-goat as presents. Not to be outdone, the remnant of the defunct Youth

Council gave him a cow. *Oha Ndom*, the women's solidarity, gave him a basket of eggs. Each group appointed a member to recite a welcome address to No Skin. The welcome addresses were so long that No Skin fell asleep in the middle of the second one. At one point he snorted noisily and woke up startled. Some brave people snickered. No Skin immediately shot the address reciter, in case any one dared to have contrary opinions about him because they had caught him napping and snoring. To put them further on the defensive, he asked:

"Do you remember the lessons you learned on the last occasion we met?"

"Yes, yes, yes," the villagers echoed.

"How many were there?" No Skin asked.

Not a soul responded. Not a soul moved. They all averted their eyes, as none of them wanted to face the consequences that would befall a wrong answer.

"You there with the tattered loin cloth," No Skin said, pointing at a man. "How many lessons were there?"

Petrified with fear, the poor villager said: "Two. I mean three! Er ... ah ... I mean, twenty-three. No, no. One. There was just one lesson ... "

Everyone thought the man was done for. They all waited tensely for the iron stick on No Skin's knee to spit fire, but it didn't. On the contrary, No Skin smiled at the man and said: "Pitiable vagabond. Here, take some of these dirty eggs and go have yourself a feast. Come, come, don't be afraid..."

What happened the very next moment proved to everyone that No Skin was truly a god. An old woman whose son had been shot by No Skin during his last visit had become desperate and had plotted to avenge him. As No Skin spoke, she had sneaked up behind him with a fufu-pounding pestle, lifted the pestle over her head and was about to let the blow fall, when No Skin suddenly turned around, snatched the pestle from her and flung it away.

"Kill me!" the woman screamed. "go ahead and kill me, whatever you are! You transparent ghost! Kill me!"

No Skin motioned to a man go drag her away. The people of Umu Madu were once again perplexed that No Skin did nothing further to punish the woman.

Umu Madu Tables A Request

At length the people of Umu Madu were able to press No Skin with their plea for a table. "Please, No Skin," they said, "we must have a table. We have not been able to enjoy a good feast in years. We now need a table more than anything else in life. Please, please, when can we have a community table?"

On hearing the pleading and begging and fawning by the people of Umu Madu, No Skin became ill-tempered. He called the villagers buffoons and baboons and bushmen and told them it was their folly and lack of imagination which made them suppose that a table such as they wanted could be quickly obtained.

"Look here," No Skin said sternly to the villagers. "It is not enough to nail pieces of wood together and call the result a table. A table is a work of both science and art. I do not have all afternoon or I would explain to you all the things that go into making a table. Just to give you an inkling I will mention a few."

No Skin then began a long recitation, which lasted the rest of the morning, all of the afternoon and well into the evening. He spoke breathlessly and in long sentences. Some villagers fell asleep and woke up hours later, and No Skin was still reciting. Some people at the back of the crowd were able to sneak away and go into the bushes to ease themselves and then return—and No Skin was still reciting the list of things that went into making a table.

Can Umu Madu Afford What It Takes To Make a Table?

"Thousands and thousands of things go into making a table," he said. A table was made of wood. There were different kinds of wood—hard, soft, smooth and knotty—not all of them suitable for making all parts of tables. Consequently anyone who wanted to construct a large table first had to know all there was to know about wood. That meant years of study. Then, of course, wood came from trees. That meant the table builder had to learn about trees. Since trees grew in forests, how could anyone hallucinate about a table without first becoming the equivalent of a forester, a botanist and a soil chemist?

No Skin then went on to explain how trees were living things which ate and breathed just like people. So anyone interested in tables had to know all there was to know about plant nutrition, about photosynthesis and transpiration, about cambium and xylem and the formation of annular rings. "The list is almost endless, my friends," No Skin concluded, shaking his head and laughing derisively. "Imagine the likeness," he added. "You people wake up from your slumber in the middle of the noonday of civilization and decide that you want a national table, and you haven't the foggiest idea what goes into making a table . . .

"On the technical side," he continued, "you need table architects and designers, engineers, carpenters and sawyers. Each of these will take years to train. Then of course they all need tools—saws, axes, chisels, planes, drills, hammers and nails. Need I go on? You still want a national table?"

"Yes, yes, yes, please," the villagers said.

"Alright then," No Skin said. "In that case let me speak briefly about other aspects of tables. As you may not know, tables didn't just come into existence on their own, fullblown, *deus ex machina*. They were invented and perfected by the people of my country through trial and error over countless generations. Although you are now going to be the beneficiaries of our thousands of years of sweat and labor, to say nothing of our ingenuity, you could not fully appreciate the art and science that are a table unless you studied the history of table-making for the last several thousand years.

"My dear friends, you cannot even permit yourselves to think of having a national table until you have studied the historical evolution of tables from pre-historic times to the present. You must learn about tables during the Stone Ages, the Early Classical Period, the Neo-Classical Period, the Dark Ages, the Bright Ages, the Enlightenment, the Victorian, and so on, and so on."

 ## To Dine Or To Die

"On the social side of things, when one of these days you are close to having a table of your own, you must learn manners and memorize an encyclopedia of etiquette that goes with dining on tables. You see, even your vocabulary has to change. 'Eating' may be a good description of the grovelling you all do now on the ground off banana leaves and raffia mats. However, when you take a meal off a proper table, with good service and etiquette what you do is not called eating. It is called dining."

"We want to dine," the villagers shouted. "Please, No Skin, we want to dine."

While the rest of the villagers were speaking in the vernacular, one man who had managed to learn a few words of No Skin's language tried to show off his knowledge. He screamed above the rest: "We want to die, No Skin, we want to die!"

No Skin picked up his iron stick and obliged the man's wish.

"Now," No Skin said, placing the smoking iron stick once more on his knee. "I have said nothing so far about the economics of tables. That was not an oversight on my part, as I am sure you realize that tables do cost money. Before you can even embark on the project, you must necessarily table a budget and decide where the money will come from to pay for the whole enterprise. Let me pause here for a minute. Are there any questions? . . ."

Not a sound came from the crowd, except that one child was snoring and another smacking his lips after suckling from his mother's breast.

"I said, are there any questions?" No Skin barked.

"No, no," the people responded. "We have no questions."

"Then you must not have understood me, or you have been sleeping," No Skin said.

In response the villagers said: "It seems like a long trip, but we are determined to make the journey. When can we start? We want to learn quickly."

 Umu Madu Prepares For An Education

The villagers were quite disappointed when No Skin told them that for those of them who were already adults there wasn't any hope of learning very much in the lifetimes they had left. It would be best to give the long training to their children.

That, in short, is how the children of Umu Madu began going to school.

After groaning with disappointment for almost half an hour, sighing and murmuring and making sad faces because they would not be able to enroll in school, the villagers of Umu Madu pleaded with No Skin to find some way of educating and training them. "Please, please, No Skin," they begged, "is there nothing at all that you can do for us adults, so that we too and not just our children can learn about tables?"

No Skin thought for a moment before replying. "Alright, my friends," he said, "be of good behavior in the meantime, and I will see what I can do for you."

That was the last thing he said that day before going away.

After several months, a syllabus came down from No Skin containing all the subjects that the children were supposed to learn. Everyone in the village was excited. At long last they were going to begin their long journey towards a Community Table. The syllabus was a thick book. It took T-and-T almost three months to finish reading it, and then people were not sure he had read it correctly because he kept contradicting himself when various villagers asked him to explain various parts of it.

What made everybody break out in cheers was the

second syllabus that No Skin had sent, a syllabus for Adult Education. "We are all going to school for the rest of our lives," they gloated. Old men shook and pumped each other's hand. Old women embraced one another in their glee and let out whoops of joy. "We will spend the rest of our lives learning about tables," they said. "Our heads will be full of book learning!"

Chapter Five

 The Chieftaincy Wars

Of course everyone in the village of Umu Madu was now a chief. Of course, of course. Man, woman or child, it made no difference. They had all gazed in THE MIRROR OF FAITH, and the mirror had shown each of them the reflection of a chief. The only exceptions were the wives who had been married and the children who had been born after No Skin's first visit. They had not gazed in the mirror. Even so, there were long discussions and bitter disputes about whether the child of a chief should not automatically inherit his parents' chieftaincy or whether the new wife of a chief should not become a chief by affinity. In the end, it was decided that there was no need to add to the number.

In the meantime, a school house was built and the children began attending classes. T-and-T became their first teacher. Very soon the adults were clamoring for their own education. T-and-T arranged to educate them. The children went to school in the morning, from the time the lizards woke up until early in the afternoon, when the flowers of the evening plant, *nsa-nsa*, opened up. The adults went from then till night fell. Everyone studied two subjects, No Skin's language, and how to count and add 1-2-3's.

What Education Did To The Traditions of Umu Madu

Because the children were spending most of their time in school, they did not learn any of the traditional skills their fathers and mothers should have been teaching them at this time. Also as time went on, the adults themselves became so involved in school and with being chiefs that they forgot or lost interest in these skills. Hardly anyone went to the farm anymore. Hardly anyone climbed palm trees anymore. The yams were unstaked; cassava plots were unweeded; and precious palm fruit rotted on the trees. Meanwhile all day long the men and women of Umu Madu idled about preening themselves like parrots, strutting about like cocks and congratulating themselves on being chiefs.

Everyone in Umu Madu became surly and ill-mannered. Wives refused to cook for their husbands, and when their husbands tried to beat them, they refused to accept the beatings. Children refused to run errands for their mothers, and when their mothers tried to punish them they ran away, mumbled disrespectfully and made faces. Young men refused to yield to their elders. Young women became very haughty and refused to get married. If a young man came with a pot of palm wine to seek a girl's hand in marriage, the girl insultingly said: "Who do you think you are, trying to marry me? You better take your wine and go home and marry yourself..."

Deep in their hearts, the people of Umu Madu were unhappy. Everyone now claimed to be a chief, so there was no emotional advantage of being chief. The old saying, "Man pass man" no longer seemed to mean anything. The new saying was, "If you chief, you chief for yourself!"

 Proper Chiefs In Proper Regalia

It was at this time that T-and-T made an announcement which made everyone's heart begin to pound again. He said that anyone who wanted to be considered a proper chief, or Chief Kpom-Kwem, had to have the proper cap, a knit cap of yellow wool, conical in shape, ending in a tassel and called *okpu odim*. Because T-and-T announced that he had only a few of these for sale, people paid very high prices for them. In the end, however, about half the people in the village bought the yellow caps.

The villagers with the yellow caps began calling themselves True Chiefs or Chief-for-True-True. Those who did not have the yellow cap were called Ordinary People or Chief-for-Mouth-Only. Arguments and fights broke out everywhere. In this era of chieftaincies, the very worst name anyone could call a villager from Umu Madu was "Ordinary Man" or "Ordinary Woman." Calling him a Chief-for-Mouth-Only was even worse. To escape the fate of being considered ordinary, people began stealing other people's caps, fomenting witchcraft, poisoning and murdering their neighbors and friends to get their caps.

T-and-T travelled again, and some weeks later returned with red caps. These he sold at twice the price of the yellow caps. People who managed to buy the red caps began calling themselves Superior Chiefs. Those who did not have the red caps became known as Inferior Chiefs. More arguments and fights. More witchcraft, poisoning and murder.

Once again T-and-T travelled. When he returned this time, the question he asked was: How could anyone call himself a chief when he marched about with his ten toes exposed, his feet unprotected from thorns, jiggers and earthworm poison. Did anyone ever see No Skin's toes?

For a chief to be a proper chief, T-and-T said, he had to have official shoes. A few villagers who managed to buy the shoes began to call themselves Genuine (Leather) Chiefs. Anyone who walked about bare-footed, no matter what type of cap he wore on his head became known as a Kanta-Feet-Chief.

Proper Chiefs in Proper Regalia

There were now all types of chiefs in the village of Umu Madu. The few who had managed to acquire the two colors of cap as well as the shoes formed an association and began calling themselves Full Power Chiefs. Those with two caps but no shoes became Paramount Chiefs. Chiefs with a red cap and shoes became Summit Chiefs. Chiefs with a yellow cap and shoes became Zenith Chief. Chiefs who had a cap and nothing else became known as Warrant Chiefs. Thus there were Red Warrant Chiefs and Yellow Warrant Chiefs. There was again a suggestion that those villagers who had acquired no insignia stop calling themselves chiefs, but this large group mounted a strong protest and came out with their machetes and spears to fight anyone who tried to un-chief them.

 Title Fights

The next thing that brought joy and then trouble to the chiefs of Umu Madu was the question of titles and nicknames. There seemed not to be enough words in the language of Umu Madu or in No Skin's language for the endless litany of titles and nicknames the chiefs of Umu Madu wanted to be called. The names of all the wild animals in the forest were soon used up, as were the names of the spirit powers in the earth and in the sky and in the waters.

First there were one-word titles like Ike, Dike, Onyiri, Igwe, Ichekiriche, Eke, Enyimiri, Ozojiri, Nkuma, Osimiri, Ototo, Akatiko, Akpu, Agu, Odumodu, Odogwo, Imerime, Ebelebe. Then people began to combine and hyphenate titles. Very soon everyone had two or three or four titles. Soon it was ten, then twenty, then forty or fifty. Umu Madu was now full of people who called themselves spiders, scorpions, boa constrictors, pythons, vipers, spitting cobras, black mambas, puff adders, lions, leopards, elephants, rhinos, hippos, Igwe N'kala, Oloro Nkuma, Ozojiri Igwe, Akpu Nku, Pagha-pagha-Yeghe-yeghe, Eke n'Egwurugwu, Ihe n'Adighi Otu n'Emeya, Bad Juju, Mba Muo Oyi, Ozo Dingba. And so on. And so on. And so on.

Life became very slow in the village. If you met a chief with 40 titles, you had to address him by all his titles or he would feel insulted and refuse to have anything to do with you. You would say: "Good morning Chief Dike-Imerime-Ototo-Amadioha-Pagha-pagha-Yeghe-yeghe-Ikemba-Odozi-obodo-Ozojiri-Igwe-Nkuma-Ike-n'ebube ..." And so on, till you recited all his titles—that is, if you could remember all of them. Then the person responded by saying "Good morning" and then calling you by all your nicknames and titles. Sometimes it took as long as twenty minutes to finish saying "Good morning."

Trouble started when the Association of Full Power Chiefs suggested that certain titles should be reserved for each class of chief. It made no sense for a Full Power chief to be nicknamed Lion or Giant or Nkuma only to have a Zenith Chief or a mere Warrant Chief call himself Lion Tamer or Giant Killer or Oloro Nkuma. However, lower echelon chiefs refused to yield their titles to anyone.

 The Strange Death of Chief Oloro Nkuma

Trouble continued when one day in order to distinguish himself from a rabble of title claimers, one villager dragged out a big ram and commenced to taunt and harangue the other villagers. "I am tired of people claiming empty titles," he shouted. "Some people call themselves Lion Tamer, yet no one has ever seen them tame a lion. Some people call themselves Oloro Nkuma, and yet no one has ever seen them swallow a rock. I am here today to show that my titles are humble but not empty: I call myself Chief Ogbu Evuru. Here's how I do it!"

Chief Oloro Evuru

Quick as a flash, the man cut off the ram's head with one stroke of his machete. While the headless animal was still writhing and thrashing about and the onlookers were still in the grip of their surprise, Chief Ogbu Evuru cut open the animal's chest and ripped out the heart. He held the bloody lump aloft for everyone to see. Then he put it in his mouth and proceeded to swallow it. When he had swallowed it down he beckoned for a drink of palm wine, then grunted and said: "There! Now when I call myself Chief Oloro Obi Evuru, you will recognize that I earned the title in front of everyone."

The Strange Death of Chief Oloro Nkuma

Thereafter a new fad began. People began to distinguish between Earned Title and Title-for-Mouth-Only. Chiefs began to go on lion hunts and snake hunts. One man swallowed the head of a viper. Several men swallowed what they said were the poison sacs of pythons and other dangerous snakes. A Chief who called himself Oloro Nkuma died in the effort to earn his title. With the cheers and jeers of the assembled village egging him on, he managed to swallow down a big stone. But the stone locked his bowels so that nothing could exit. Purgative medicine only made the matter worse. He died about a week later. Not long afterwards another man who wanted to be called Oloro Nkuma swallowed a much smaller stone. People jeered at him however and called him a pebble swallower.

And so the fights and contests continued in the village of Umu Madu over who was what type of chief. Alliances were formed, broken and re-formed. Machetes, spears and poisoned arrows were in great use, as were nsi, otumokpo, onunu, and every imaginable type of "means." These fights became known in history as the Chieftaincy Wars of Umu Madu. The people of Umu Madu were so busy fighting these wars, that they almost forgot about No Skin. Then one day No Skin returned.

 No Skin Explains The Fighting

Battered and bedraggled, the chiefs and would-be chiefs of Umu Madu, first class, second class and no class, Zenith, Paramount and whatever, stumbled and staggered out to the market clearing to meet No Skin. Some of them thought that he would settle the disputes and put an end to the fighting. They were disappointed.

No Skin instead told all of them that they were learning one of the important lessons of civilization: "You have to fight for what you believe." For what was the use of faith if one was not prepared to fight and die for it. Besides, No Skin said, the world was ruled by a principle known as Survival of the Fittest. That was why in the forest big animals gored or trampled or clawed small animals, and in the ocean big fish ate little fish.

The only thing No Skin did not like about their fighting was that they did it at random. "You cannot simply run helter-skelter with a machete," he said, "and whack everyone you see. You must organize your fighting. You must learn to fight pitched battles. In time you must organize yourselves into armies. You never heard of armies? In that case I must make a note to include military training in the syllabus for your children. An army is a disciplined force of professional fighters, people who have been trained to fight and are equipped with good weapons and know how to use them. Organize! Organize! Organize! The days of indiscriminate butchery are over. You must learn to kill your enemies scientifically."

"What do we do with the people we overcome or capture in battle, if we do not kill them?" some of the villagers wanted to know.

"Tie them up and turn them over to me," No Skin said. "I'll take care of them. By the way, I will reward you handsomely for your prisoners, especially if they are young and healthy."

 T-and-T Becomes Chief Of All Chiefs

Before he departed that afternoon, No Skin wrote down everyone's name and what class of chief he was. He then had the entire assembly recognize T-and-T as Chief of All Chiefs. From that day onwards, he said, T-and-T was his representative to them and their representative to him.

"Finally," No Skin said, "because you have been such good people, I have a present for you, which I am sure will make all of you happy. I will donate a table to you for your feasts. This way you do not have to wait 20 or

30 years for your children to finish their training before you get a table of your own. The table I will give you is second-hand, but I assure you it is of the best quality known to civilization. Be sure to use it well."

The people cheered and cheered and danced for joy.

Chapter Six

Na waya kwanu for the village of Umu Madu, a village where everyone used to live in peace and have frequent feasts in harmony. Now half the population was gone, killed in the numerous wars or bound as prisoners of war and handed over to No Skin. Of those who remained, most were battered and bewildered and had made caricatures of themselves trying to be chiefs. All because Umu Madu wanted to eat on tables.

In the old, old days, which everyone had almost forgotten, the people of Umu Madu used to be fiercely independent and self-respecting. "Is your *nyash* the door to my house?" one villager would ask another, if he felt he had been insulted. The obvious answer to the question was of course "No," and to that the insulted villager would further add: "Then what makes you think you can insult or disrespect me?" Now, however, independence and self-respect had left the village of Umu Madu. Everyone was concerned with surviving and getting ahead, and if getting ahead meant licking some else's *nyash*, the people of Umu Madu were prepared to smack their lips and lick their way up. It seemed that everyone was now following the proverb of the pariah dog which said: "It's always wisest to walk behind those who have had a lot to eat, because if something doesn't come out of them one end it is bound to come out the other end."

How The Tradition Of Sending Congratulatory Messages Started

The day after No Skin's departure, T-and-T's compound was filled with delegations of congratulators, well-wishers, nyash-lickers and flatterers of all kinds. Messengers and messages came in from everywhere. People trampled, shoved and elbowed one another for the opportunity to stand before The Chief of All Chiefs and offer their loyalty and service.

During the next several weeks, many important events occurred in the village of Umu Madu:

The people began building a palace, the first one ever, for The Chief of All Chiefs. One hundred of the strongest young men in the village were constituted into a Palace Guard to protect him, and enforce the rules he made. Twelve chiefs were appointed as his special advisers—six Full Power, three Paramount, and the other three drawn on a rotational basis from the remaining miscellany of chieftaincy ranks. The Chief of All Chiefs selected 12 titles for himself, which no one else was permitted to use. Ten new wives were added to his former two, to give him a total of twelve. He could have married more if he wanted to because people were eager to become his in-laws and thereby give themselves an entree to the palace, and as insurance against the hazards and vicissitudes of life.

Anyone found disobeying one of the new rules was thrashed soundly by the Palace Guard—if he was an ordinary villager or Chief-for-Mouth-Only. If the miscreant was one of the other petty chiefs, he was demoted one rank and had to forfeit a cap or his shoes.

Umu Madu Gets a Table On The Installment Plan

By far the most significant event of the season was the arrival of the first installment of No Skin's Old Table. This was the foundation segment, and it had the people of Umu Madu clasping their hands, shaking their heads and snapping their fingers in wonder and amazement at the size and magnificence of what was before them. They had never seen anything like it, and could not even begin to imagine how it was part of a table. Nevertheless, they followed instructions and planted it firmly in the ground.

Soon, a new installment of the Table began to arrive each week. The villagers scurried about feverishly, figuring out how the various parts fit together. It was a truly complicated table. Very soon they found it necessary to build bamboo ladders and scaffolds. More than a few men fell off the ladders or scaffolds or work platforms and broke their legs or backs. Two broke their necks.

When the last component of the Table was in place, the people of Umu Madu stood back and tilted their heads to behold what they had constructed. It was not the kind of table they had expected, with legs and one flat surface; it was a tower as high as a tall tree; it was table-times-seven, that is, a table on top of a table on top of another table, all the way to the seventh layer.

A day was set for the inaugural feast on this table. Preparations were made. For weeks the village talked of little else than the feast and did little else than prepare it.

The Termites' Feast

On the night before the feast, disaster struck. The whole edifice collapsed. At first, everyone thought "sabotage," but what malcontent would do such a shameful thing. No Skin's last coming had pacified everyone.

No Skin became red in the face and paced back and forth angrily when he arrived for the Inaugural Feast and found the Table lying on its side. "Can't you blasted baboons do anything right?" he said angrily, as he went about inspecting the damage to the ancient table. "We have used this for generations and never had any trouble with it," he said.

No Skin appointed a commission of inquiry to look into the causes of the collapse and recommend a solution. After No Skin had left, the villagers themselves, with T-and-T's blessing, decided to engage a famous seer to look into the matter.

The answer from both investigations was the same, more or less. The seer said that the table had collapsed because of something in the soil. The Land was displeased with the foreign object planted into it without proper sacrifices. "Termites!" No Skin's commission of inquiry reported back. The table was made of soft wood, which the lively termites in the soil of Umu Madu had found excellent eating.

With No Skin visiting frequently and sometimes staying overnight in a Rest House, which Umu Madu constructed for him, the villagers were able to build a new foundation for the table, this time made of native wood. In about a year, the table was standing again in its magnificence, more than a little rough on the base, where the natives had shown their lack of experience, and planks were badly planed, and corners didn't fit and nails missed their marks. A new date was set for the Inaugural Celebration.

This time the celebration was a success. There was dancing and feasting for weeks. At the height of the celebration, No Skin and T-and-T standing at the highest layer of the table, held up their joined hands to the crowd. Jubilant cheers rang from every throat. Then the speeches began. The day was called a day of destiny, a new day, a new dawn, a new beginning, an august and auspicious occasion, a day fraught with challenges and opportunities. Every chief worth his cap made a long speech. Women danced. Young girls danced. Men in masquerades danced. Acrobats leaped and somersaulted. The Palace Guard drilled. The newly recruited regiment of the Table Guards marched. The children paraded in their new school uniforms, making their fathers and mothers very proud. A new proclamation, which was called a Constitution, was read. It would govern everyone's behavior at all future feasts. People cheered everything that happened that day, even mistakes that were made.

Umu Madu Un-invents The Law Of Gravity: What Goes Up Does Not Necessarily Come Down

It was several months after the Inaugural Celebration before some people began to notice that they were not entirely happy with the way the table was constructed, how and where people were seated and how the food was shared. Some began to ask questions: Was this not supposed to be a community feast on a community table? Had they not decided to build a Community Table so they could all eat together? What No Skin had given them was not a single table but seven tables stacked on top of another.

There was a vertical tube in the center of the edifice through which ran a spiral stairway. The entrance to this stairway was marked "Private. No Admittance!" Only T-and-T and the Full Power Chiefs could use this stairway. All the food eaten at the feast was also carried via this stairway to be blessed at the top by T-and-T and his Special Advisers.

Why did the food have to be carried to the top and

then brought down again? Because the Constitution said that the people of Umu Madu were forbidden to eat food that had not been blessed. Naturally the food could best be blessed by T-and-T and the Special Advisers, since their position at the highest table placed them nearest to God.

There was also a second set of stairways. Actually these were shaky ladders by which the lower echelon chiefs could ascend from one level to the next.

The Feast Becomes A Party—Eating Becomes Chopping—Fufu Becomes National Cake

According to the Constitution, food was no longer called food but "cake" or "pie," even though the people of Umu Madu still ate fufu, garri, or jollof rice. (This is why, even today, the people of Umu Madu constantly talk of getting a piece of national pie or complain about not getting their share of the national cake.)

Eating was no longer called eating but chopping.

The feasts of Umu Madu were no longer called feasts. They were called parties instead. In the old, old days, when the village of Umu Madu used to have merry community feasts on the ground, anyone who happened to be nearby, even strangers, was invited to "join the feast." In the new order, the invitation became "Join the party first, that is, if you want to chop some of the national cake." In fact, to be admitted to a table above Level One, you had to show your "party and registration card" to one of the Table Guards.

The Table Guards kept law and order (and quite a bit of the cake) during the feasts. They carried big sticks and their instructions were to crack the head of anyone who became disorderly or loud during the feast, especially anyone who tried to leave his table for a higher one without proper authorization.

After the food had been blessed, The Chief of All Chiefs and the Full Power Chiefs on Table Seven chose what they wanted. The remainder was carried or shoved down to Table Six, where the assorted excellencies and highnesses who belonged to this level satisfied themselves. What was not consumed there or trampled or hidden went to Table Five. And so on and so forth to the lowest table.

However, by the time the blessed food had reached Table Two, only bare bones and gristle were left of the meat. All sorts of chiefs had poked their searching fingers into the soup and jollof rice and extracted the meat. So the many villagers who ate at the lowest and on the ground—yes, some villagers still ate on the ground and were quite angry and noisy about it—fought one another for the scraps and leftovers that came down from above. In time these unfortunate people came to be known as the "party rank and vile." Sometimes they would try to storm up the ladders to the higher tables, and it was up to the Table Guards to block the stairs and crack some heads.

Umu Madu Learns Of Trickle-Down Theory

As time went on discontent grew. All the food for the party went up to be blessed, but blessed little of it came down again. The situation reminded people of all the delegations which T-and-T had taken to see No Skin. The rank and vile clamored for more of the National Cake. They claimed to have become mere spectators at the feasts. After some time their constant clamoring and their threats to knock down the table became annoying to the excellencies dining at the top. Squads of Table Guards were sent down to crack heads and restore order. However, there were so many heads to crack that the guards soon became tired of cracking them. Also, the guards became surly because while they were busy cracking heads they themselves could not enjoy the feast. What to do? After a while, the rank and vile were no longer content to make unruly noises and shake their fists in anger. They began to shake the table.

    T-and-T appealed to No Skin for help. As always, No Skin had the perfect solution. He called the first part of the solution "Operation Hope." He told T-and-T and the Full Power Chiefs: "Remember your own proverb, which says that no condition is permanent. These wretched people at the bottom of the heap must be made to feel that their deprivation is not permanent, even though it may be. So you must give them a little bit of cake and a lot of hope. Hope makes people who are downcast look up and people who are downbeat upbeat."

    No Skin further explained that this was the essence of the theory known as Trickle-Down Theory. Something had to trickle down to the people at the bottom. It didn't matter what or how much as long as it trickled down regularly. "So when you hear them clamoring below," No Skin said, "throw down a few scraps, and you will immediately notice two things happen. First they will trample and kill one another fighting for the scraps, meanwhile leaving you to continue your feast in peace. Secondly, they will be fighting one another to get into position to catch the next morsel you discard from above. Thus, when they look up at you, in spite of all the embezzling and gormandizing they can see you doing, their eyes will be filled with hope and greed rather than with envy—hope that they will be fortunate and catch the next scrap you decide to throw down. That, you see, is how Trickle-Down Theory works, and why it is so successful."

Representative Chopping Comes to Umu Madu

"However," No Skin continued, "the best way to control the rank and vile is through a hoax of democratic representation. Have the rank and vile conduct free elections to select people to represent them on the higher tables. Once people feel represented at the feast, they don't mind so much anymore that they themselves get nothing so long as their representatives are doing—what's your word for it now?—the chopping."

That was how free elections and democratic representation came to Umu Madu. The whole village was divided into electoral districts. There was a long campaign during which the chiefs from the upper tables came down and made long speeches and "dashed" out some of the booty they had been secreting away from all the

Representative "Chopping" Comes to Umu Madu

feasts of yesteryear. The rank and vile cheered. They were very glad and proud to have a voice in selecting representatives to chop national cake on their behalf. "My vote put him up there," they congratulated themselves, when they observed the chopping going on at the high tables. "If it weren't for me, he wouldn't be up there now chopping."

The whole situation came under control again, just as No Skin had predicted. The chiefs on the upper tables were gormandizing legitimately as representatives of the rank and vile. They mastered the Tickle-Down Theory and made sure scraps always fell to the lower tables to keep the rank and vile ever hopeful and fighting among themselves. From time to time, T-and-T called for new elections, and the Representative Chiefs of Umu Madu went down among the rank and vile to renew their mandate to keep chopping. They came down with rare tidbits of previously concealed national cake and pie, which they dashed to the cheering and flattering rank and vile. For the little "dash" they received and for bigger scraps they were promised, the rank and vile were prepared to commit arson, pillage, mayhem and murder in order to get their preferred representatives elected. Some formed themselves into marauding gangs with names like Party Faithful, Party Vanguard, Party Stalwarts and Youth Brigands. These went about holding rallies and terrorizing the loin cloths off their rivals.

The Ladder Of Opportunity

After some time there was an innovation in the system for which credit did not go to No Skin. This was the purely local invention known as the Ladder of Opportunity. A Ladder of Opportunity, which only the Representative Chiefs could carry, had magical qualities, among them the fact that it was so thin that it fit tidily into a pocket and it was invisible except to the person to whom it was being thrown.

The Ladder of Opportunity created a road where the sign said "No Road." It opened doors marked "No Admittance." It enabled a user to leap-frog from the back to the front of a long line of waiting people. It had the power to make a Table Guard temporarily blind or could force him to look the other way, while the user went past the gate the Table Guard was supposed to block. "As man know man," a Representative Chief could use the Ladder of Opportunity to send goodies secretly to his friends and relatives or to people he regarded as his constituents. The old saying used to be: "Where there is a will, there is a way." In those days in the village of Umu Madu, the saying was: "Where there is a Ladder of Opportunity there is a way."

No Skin Departs—
Umu Madu Is Given Back To Itself

Things continued this way for years. Then one day No Skin decided that he was tired and bored and fed up with the people of Umu Madu. He asked T-and-T to announce the biggest feast ever so he could take formal leave of the people.

During this feast, many of the chiefs made long, boring speeches. Women danced. Girls danced. School children marched in their uniforms. The Palace Guard paraded. The Table Guards drilled. Masqueraders pranced around while acrobats somersaulted.

In the middle of the feast No Skin announced that he was giving the people of Umu Madu back to themselves. He had taught them what they needed to know and now he was going home. He had rescued them from their erstwhile bestial nature, taught them how to be like people and used faith to make it possible for them to become chiefs. Their lawlessness and indiscipline he had turned into meek obedience and discipline. "*Bonitas disciplina scientia,*" he said in a language which none of them had ever heard before and no one could translate. Above everything else, he had taught them how to eat on a table rather than grovel on the ground. And now he was leaving behind for their benefit a most sacred bequest—a table which had served his own people for generations, which he hoped would serve them for as many generations in the future. All they had to do was wax and polish and keep it in good repair.

"Umu Madu," No Skin proclaimed, "you are free and on your own!"

The cheers that came from the throats of the crowd made fourteen people deaf—they were so loud. No one had ever seen or heard so much rejoicing before. The people of Umu Madu spent two full days thanking No Skin for his generosity to them, for allowing them to look in THE MIRROR OF TRUTH for a correct understanding of their true nature, but especially for transforming them from that nature through the dazzling MIRROR OF FAITH. How could they ever thank him enough, the people of Umu Madu asked, for teaching them obedience and how to fight in an organized way. What words were there to express their gratitude to him for the syllabus he had drawn up for the education of their children and themselves.

As for the Table he had given them, words were not enough to thank him, the people of Umu Madu told No Skin. So as a sacred memento of their eternal gratitude to him, they solemnly swore to him before all the jujus of their village that they would never, never change the syllabus of education he had designed for them, nor would they ever build a table that was not a true copy of the one he had given them. They swore seven times for themselves, and then seven more times for all their unborn children.

No Skin was so touched by this effusion of gratitude that a large teardrop fell from his left eye. Following his example, about ten top-ranking chiefs, including T-and-T, shed tears to mark the occasion. Handshakes and hugs were exchanged all around, and then No Skin departed for the final time.

That day of No Skin's departure became known in the history of Umu Madu as Return-to-Self Day. It is still celebrated every year.

Chapter Seven

Umu Madu Today—Learning and Chopping

Could the people fo Umu Madu govern themselves? Had they learned discipline? Would faith save them from their fate? Or was it education that would save them? Could they be trusted to maintain order and good manners while feasting, chopping, quaffing and guzzling around No Skin's ancient table? Would they wax and polish The Table regularly and otherwise keep it in good repair, so that it would continue to serve them into the indefinite future?

The destiny of Umu Madu was in question from the beginning. For the first few years after No Skin left, the answers were positive more or less. Chopping the National Cake continued unabated, but it was not much worse than before. The only difference was that the feasts went from being frequent to being continuous. At first there were morning feasts, afternoon feasts and night feasts. Then there was just one feast, which never ended. During the feasts everyone got to chop a little bit, even though the rank and vile on Table One and the ground still got only bare bones and pot scrapings.

Then there was trouble at the top. The Representative

Choppers on Table Five, Six and Seven were no longer content to chop and let chop among themselves. Dissension arose among them. Factions formed. Alliances formed among the various factions. The National Choppers Party allied with the Progressive Choppers in an effort to wrest control of the feast from the United Choppers and their allies, the Voracious Choppers and the Omnivorous Choppers. Many a feast ended in fisticuffs, and it was quite a sight to see the Chief Choppers of Umu Madu punching, kicking, rolling on the floor, whacking each other with cooked, juicy leg-of-goat or femur-of-cow, or dousing each other with overnight palm wine. Pots, basins and plates were knocked over in the fracas, and that became the only way for food or drink to trickle down. Sometimes, though, combatants fell over the edge of the platform to the cheers and jeers of the rank and vile below, who would interrupt their own fighting long enough to stomp the fallers to death, if they had not already broken their necks in their fall. Thus the fights of the Chief Choppers at the Upper Tables became a source of entertainment for the hapless rank and vile.

New Elections

When things were truly out of hand, T-and-T dissolved the feast and sent everyone home for a month, so that fresh elections could be held. The Representative Chopping Chiefs dismounted from the Upper Tables to campaign among the rank and vile. The campaign was noisy and full of accusations about who was chopping most of the National Cake, who deserved most to chop it and who was most responsible for the rank and vile's getting neither crumb nor trickle. In the end, those who handed out the biggest bribes or made the most outrageous promises won the elections to the Upper Tables.

As soon as the feast re-commenced, the losers of the election accused the winners of rigging and cheating and frauding. Fighting broke out anew among the Representative Chopping Chiefs. The fighters forgot many proverbs they should have remembered, among them:

"No condition is permanent."

"If you want to eat hot pepper soup, you take it slowly and a little bit at a time."

"It may be better to have nothing to eat than to eat so much that your big belly causes you to collapse on the wayside."

"When death is stalking a pariah dog, he loses even his best sense—his sense of smell."

Monki De Work, Baboon De Chop

There were uprisings and downfalls. The Chief Choppers continued to fall off the edge of the table. The rank and vile continued to rise in riot. The Palace Guards and the Table Guards had their hands full as they tried to control the table-rockers above and the table-rockers below. Then one day the Guards decided they had had enough of this monkey business. They called it "monkey business" because they said later that the situation reminded them of the proverb: "Monki de work, baboon de chop." The Guards were tired of being the monkeys, so they set upon the chopping baboons and taught them a lesson.

T-and-T and most of the highest ranking chiefs were sent to join the ancestors. The rest of the chiefs fled from their lofty perches and did their best to get lost among the rank and vile. However the rank and vile ferreted out the escapees (it was easy to tell them from the size of their stomachs) and either turned them over to the Guards or stomped their big bellies until the truth came out of them from both ends.

The Guards called a big feast, the biggest anyone had seen so far. It began with everyone dancing merrily on the ground, including the Guards who wanted to show everyone how humble they were. After the dancing however, the Guards climbed to the Upper Tables and from there told the people that they were henceforth to be called the Supreme Redemptive Guards of National Cake. As all members of the rank and vile could see, everything was again under control, and no member of the rank and vile had anything to fear, although the Supreme Redemptive Guards would not tolerate any unnecessary noise-making while they were busy guarding the National Cake.

Things settled down quite a bit. The Guards were no-nonsense people. They were brutal in the teaching of lessons and the administration of discipline. There were now two types of people in the village of Umu Madu—military and civilian. The military were militant and the civilians were expected to be civil. Since the former Guards were now busy administering the feast and safeguarding the National Cake on the Upper Tables, new guards were recruited from the rank and vile to keep order during the feasts.

 The Supreme Redemptive Guards—Were They Guarding Or Chopping The National Cake?

For some time it was not quite clear whether the Supreme Redemptive Guards were guarding or chopping most of the National Cake. However, since the Trickle-Down Theory seemed to have begun operating once again, the rank and vile gave them the benefit of every doubt. What did it matter whether they did more chopping than guarding so long as something trickled down to the people below? So, all in all, if the people of Umu Madu were not altogether content or happy, they were resigned.

Then the trickle in Trickle-Down slowed. Then it stopped altogether. It became obvious that the Supreme Redemptive Guards had become like the Representative Chiefs, whom they displaced. They were doing more chopping than guarding. The rank and vile began to grumble, then to rock and agitate the old Table. They even set a few fires. The New Guards were dispatched to crack the head of the trouble makers and pacify them.

However, as soon as the commotion died down, one member of the Supreme Redemptive Guards, the one who was in charge of training the New Guards, mounted a surgical operation against his comrades and sent most of them to join the ancestors. Then he announced that from that day onwards he alone was the Chief Guardian of the National Cake. This important turn of events (or tables) came to be known in history as "The Changing of the Guards."

For a long time, the Guards continued to change. Umu Madu's feasts went through cycles of guard-chop-change, which continues till this day.

Na waya kwanu for Umu Madu!

 **The Education Continues**

Meanwhile the children and youth of Umu Madu continued to receive an education strictly according to the syllabus No Skin had drawn up for them. The oath their parents had sworn never to receive any other kind of education was supposed to pass from generation to generation. First, they received infantile education. Next they received primary education. After that they attended purely secondary schools. After that came tertiary school, then quartenary school, and so on and so forth all the way to duodevigintenary school

Some schools gave high education; others gave higher education. Some offered education at ordinary levels;

others offered it at advanced levels. Sometimes the education was specific; at other times it was general. Students who had not learned anything specific received the General Certificate of Education. (Quite a few received Forged Certificates of Education.)

After some time UMEC (Umu Madu Examinations Council) was set up to administer exams and as often as possible leak them to prospective candidates.

Students who passed the first set of examinations set by UMEC earned the First-School-Leaving-Certificate. After the First School Leaving Certificate came the Second, then the Third and then the Never-School-Leaving Certificate.

Education was like water to the children of Umu Madu. They were always talking of "thirsting" for it. Thus, after certificates, students who thirsted for more education studied for diplomas—high, higher, and highest. After diplomas the brightest of the children of Umu Madu had an option of being educated to a degree—first degree, second degree or third degree. Those who were truly *in extremis* received something called the "terminal degree."

What did the children of Umu Madu actually learn for all their education? "Book" was their answer. The children of Umu Madu learn book, learn book so-tay bookpage become blank! They were hypnotized savants, who enjoyed amazing one another and their mothers by reciting whole books, including some that were up to four hundred pages long. They were so enthralled by book-learning that everything they felt or knew came from a book.

 ## Specialization: Learning More About Less

When all the general aspects of everything that had anything to do with tables in No Skin's syllabus had been committed to memory, the children of Umu Madu began to probe deeply into specific aspects of tables. In short, they began to specialize. Soon there were specialists on everything—table legs, table wax, table manners, nails, pegs, termites, the history of tables, tables as metaphor in literature, wood, aphids, forestry, soil chemistry, and so on, and so on, and so on. Specialists learned more and more about less and less until they learned everything there was to learn about nothing.

Education became so complicated that the children of Umu Madu forgot why they were in school in the first place. Some began saying that the real purpose of education was not to learn anything but to learn how to learn.

This was called meta-education. The brightest of the youth began to specialize in Meta-Education. After that some of the very, very brightest pursued Meta-Meta-Education. They learned how-to-learn how-to-learn. And that was not the end of their specialization either!

A whole generation had now grown up who had known nothing but school, because their parents had enrolled them at the earliest possible age. Many of the older people, who had gazed in No Skin's MIRROR OF TRUTH and MIRROR OF FAITH, had joined the ancestors. A new order began to emerge among the people of Umu Madu. The older people had prided themselves on their chieftaincy titles. The younger people now prided themselves mainly on Book. If you were a Chief and also sabi book, then you were truly something. So, some of the sons of the old chiefs, now dead, began to call themselves Princes or Chiefs-by-Birth. If in addition they had been recruited by the Guards, they also waved academic, military and other titles around. Thus, a young notable might introduce himself as Chief-the-Honorable-Doctor-Professor-Birgadier-General-Et-Cetera-Et-Cetera Odozi Obodo of Umu Madu.

Epilogue

 The Chopping Continues

The feasts of Umu Madu, dreary affairs as they now are, are still held on that relic of a table bequeathed by No Skin uncountable years ago. Parts of the table have rotted. Planks have warped and pulled out of place in the hot sun. Termites have done their duty on much of the wood, and there are holes everywhere. The entire structure creaks, wobbles and lurches dangerously. With the slightest wind it threatens to keel over. Numerous over-eager climbers have been known to fall off the ladders that lead from one level to another. Meanwhile the people of Umu Madu have continued to repair, buttress and shore-up the table as if it were a sacred heirloom which they cannot or dare not replace.

From time to time a villager who has had too much to eat or drink suggests that Umu Madu should design and build its own table. A spirited discussion usually follows such a suggestion, but in the end everyone says: "The table, just like the wheel, has already been invented; there is no need trying to re-invent it." Furthermore, frequent delegations have travelled to No Skin's country to shop for other second-hand tables. The delegations usually stay a long time, squander the money they were given or hide it in secret bank accounts and come home empty-handed.

Will the people of Umu Madu ever design and build their own table? Can they? Usually in the village of Umu Madu, if a young bride does not show pregnancy after some months of marriage, people teasingly begin to ask her: "Is it that the barber doesn't know how to do his job, or isn't his razor sharp?" Perhaps that is the question Umu Madu should now answer.

Meanwhile, the children are still sentenced to Perpetual Bookish Education, which is now universal and compulsory.

As for the control of the feast, the guarding of the National Cake and the determination of how it is chopped and by whom and how much is allowed to trickle down to the rank and vile, controllers and guardians, both civilian and military, have been coming and going like the seasons. In the meantime the chopping continues . . . the chopping continues . . . the chopping continues.

Afterword

TABLES is a contemporary fable which, in the tradition of such well known tales as "Why Mosquitoes Buzz in People's Ears" and "Why the Tortoise's Shell Is Patched," attempts to explain why things are the way they are in our world. It is a gift from me and my generation to my children and their generation.

Many of the folktales we joyously re-tell today were invented a long time ago by elders who felt a need "to make sense" of their world for themselves and their children. But alas, my generation "has gone to school," and asked by our children to explain the world we live in, we tend to create windstorms of political, economic or sociological verbiage. TABLES is a modest effort to see the myth and fable in our times.

In some parts, the book goes beyond explanation to parody and satire. In other parts, it is a book of *gburu bara uru, gburu bara okukpu* (cut into flesh, cut into bone) and is filled with the spirit of *pagha-pagha yeghe-yeghe*. In general, however, it is only a book of "as I sidon de look, na so I see-am."

It sweet me to write-am. I hope it go sweet you to read-am.

Chief Efanim Ekeh
Inyanga the First of Uwa Dum